D1370598

DISCARD

HELEN V. GRIFFITH

Dream Meadow

Pictures by NANCY BARNET

Greenwillow Books
New York

Colored pencils were used for the full-color art.
The text type is Schneidler.
Text copyright © 1994 by Helen V. Griffith
Illustrations copyright © 1994 by Nancy Barnet
Greenwillow Books, a division of William Morrow & Company, Inc.,
1350 Avenue of the Americas, New York, NY 10019.
Printed in Hong Kong by South China Printing Company (1988) Ltd.
First Edition   10 9 8 7 6 5 4 3 2 1

Library of Congress Cataloging-in-Publication Data

Griffith, Helen V.
Dream meadow / by Helen V. Griffith;
pictures by Nancy Barnet.
p.   cm.
Summary: An old woman and her dog share a dream of the days
when they were younger, until they leave this world together.
ISBN 0-688-12293-0 (trade).   ISBN 0-688-12294-9 (lib. bdg.)
[1. Old age—Fiction. 2. Death—Fiction. 3. Dogs—Fiction.]
I. Barnet, Nancy, ill.   II. Title.
PZ7.G8823Dr   1994
[E]—dc20   93-18175   CIP   AC

FOR FOXY
—H. V. G.

FOR BRIAN, KATHY,
AND KRISTEN,
AND FOR THE GROUP,
WITH THANKS
—N. B.

The old lady spends her days in a rocking chair, but she doesn't rock anymore.
She needs help to walk and she eats hardly anything, and sometimes she doesn't know her own daughter, even though she lives with her.

The dog lying by her side is old, too. She is almost blind and nearly deaf. She walks a little and eats a little, but most of her time is spent dreaming by the rocking chair.
The daughter calls them her two old ladies.

Every now and then the dog pulls herself up and lays her chin on the old lady's knee. The old lady puts her hand on the old dog's head and whispers very low, "Good girl. Good old Frisky." And Frisky's tail wags a little wag.

Then the daughter shakes her head and says, "My two old ladies."

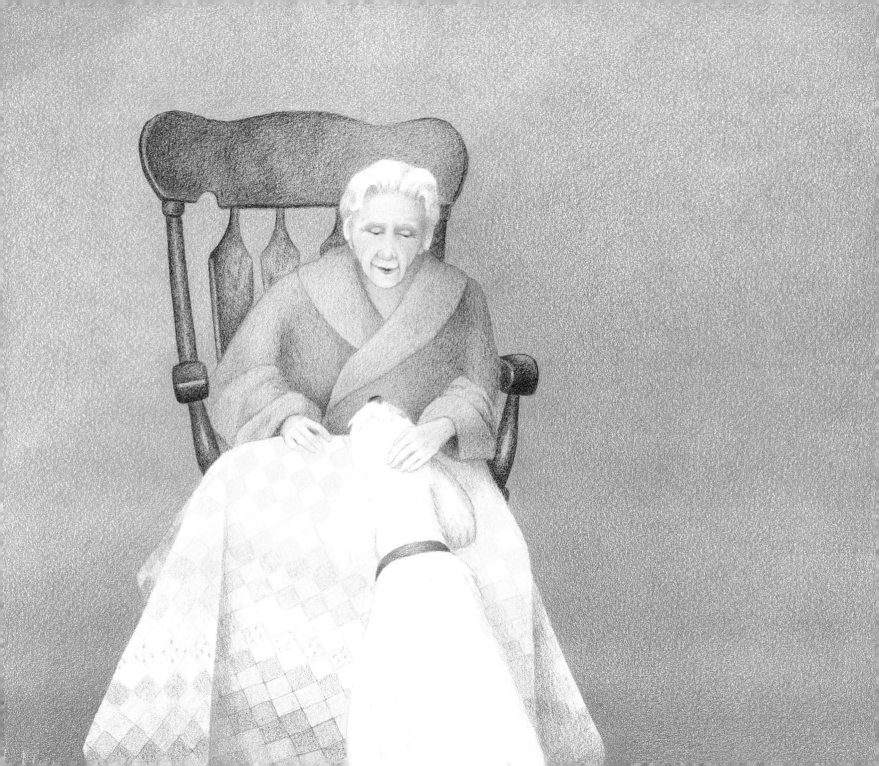

The old lady's name is Jane, but as a girl she was called Jenny. Jenny could skip and jump, and she could run as fast as the wind could blow. The old lady dreams about that a lot. She isn't quite asleep, but she's not quite awake, either.
In her waking dream there is a meadow with tall green grass and yellow flowers and clouds of orange butterflies.

Jenny runs in the sunshine and the soft, blowing air, and sometimes in her dream she calls, "Here, Frisky." And that's when Frisky puts her chin on the old lady's knee, and Jane whispers, "Good old dog."

The dog has her dreams, too. Frisky is young again then, like Jenny, and as lively as when she was first named Frisky. She tears through the meadow, snapping at the flowers and leaping up toward the butterflies, but every so often she stops and looks around and tilts her head to listen.
She is waiting for something, but she's not sure yet what it is.

Sometimes Frisky doesn't want to come back from her dream. It's good to feel like a puppy again. It's good to be able to see and to hear and to run without hurting. Sometimes Frisky wants to go on running and running across the grassy meadow faster and faster until she runs straight up into the sky. But she never does it, because she remembers the old lady dozing in her chair.

So Frisky draws herself back from her dream meadow, and she touches the old lady's hand with her cold, dry nose. Then Jane smiles a tiny smile and says, "Good old Frisky."

The daughter looks at the old dog. She sees her mother's tiny smile. "My two old ladies," she says, and she slowly shakes her head.

A day comes when Jenny is picking flowers in her dream meadow, and she is suddenly so full of life and energy that she has to run. She races across the meadow, letting the wind take the flowers from her hands. She feels that if she runs fast enough she will run straight up into the sky. Jenny laughs as she runs, and she calls, "Here, Frisky. Here, Frisky."

The old dog drags herself up and
puts her chin on the old lady's knee.
Jane doesn't move her hand. She
doesn't whisper, "Good old girl."
Frisky licks the cool, unmoving
hand and drops back down beside
the rocking chair.

Gently Frisky drifts into her old dream of green grass and yellow flowers and orange butterflies. But the meadow isn't a dream anymore. It's real, and Jenny is there, skimming over the grass, moving faster than the wind.

Now Frisky knows what she has been waiting for. She barks loudly and races after Jenny.

And together they run straight up into the sky.

E
GRIFF

Griffith, Helen V.

Dream meadow.

√545832

DATE			